Philip Roth

The Prague Orgy

In the 1990s Philip Roth won America's four major literary awards in succession: the National Book Critics Circle Award for *Patrimony* (1991), the PEN/Faulkner Award for *Operation Shylock* (1993), the National Book Award for *Sabbath's Theater* (1995), and the Pulitzer Prize in fiction for *American Pastoral* (1997). He won the Ambassador Book Award of the English-Speaking Union for *I Married a Communist* (1998); in the same year he received the National Medal of Arts at the White House. Previously he won the National Book Critics Circle Award for *The Counterlife* (1986) and the National Book Award for his first book, *Goodbye, Columbus* (1959). In 2000 he published *The Human Stain*, concluding a trilogy that depicts the ideological ethos of postwar America. For *The Human Stain* Roth received his second PEN/Faulkner Award as well as Britain's W. H. Smith Award for the Best Book of the Year. In 2001 he received the highest award of the American Academy of Arts and Letters, the Gold Medal in Fiction, given every six years "for the entire work of the recipient."

D0059571

INTERNATIONAL

BOOKS BY Philip Roth

ZUCKERMAN BOOKS

The Ghost Writer
Zuckerman Unbound
The Anatomy Lesson
The Prague Orgy

The Counterlife

American Pastoral
I Married a Communist
The Human Stain

ROTH BOOKS

The Facts
Deception
Patrimony
Operation Shylock

KEPESH BOOKS

The Breast
The Professor of Desire
The Dying Animal

OTHER BOOKS

Goodbye, Columbus • Letting Go
When She Was Good • Portnoy's Complaint
Our Gang • The Great American Novel
My Life as a Man • Reading Myself and Others
Sabbath's Theater • Shop Talk

The Prague Orgy

Philip Roth

The Prague Orgy

Vintage International

Vintage Books

A Division of Random House, Inc.

New York

FIRST VINTAGE INTERNATIONAL EDITION, JANUARY 1996

Library of Congress Cataloging-in-Publication Data
Roth, Philip.
The Prague orgy / by Philip Roth. — 1st Vintage International
ed.
p. cm.
ISBN 0-679-74903-9
I. Title.
PS3568.O855P68 1996
813'.54—dc20 95-24898
CIP

Manufactured in the United States of America
10 9 8 7 6 5

The Prague Orgy

... from Zuckerman's notebooks

New York, Jan. 11, 1976

Y our novel," he says, "is absolutely one of the five or
six books of my life."

"You must assure Mr. Sisovsky," I say to his companion,
"that he has flattered me enough."

"You have flattered him enough," she tells him. A
woman of about forty, pale eyes, broad cheekbones, dark,
severely parted hair—a distraught, arresting face. One blue
vein bulges dangerously in her temple as she perches at the
edge of my sofa, quite still. In black like Prince Hamlet.
Signs of serious wear at the seat of the black velvet skirt

3

of her funereal suit. Her fragrance is strong, her stockings laddered, her nerves shot.

He is younger, perhaps by ten years: thick-bodied, small, sturdy, with a broad, small-nosed face that has the ominous potency of a gloved fist. I see him lowering the brow and breaking doors down with it. Yet the longish hair is the hair of the heartthrob, heavy, silky hair of an almost Oriental darkness and sheen. He wears a gray suit, a faintly luminous fabric, the jacket tailored high under the arms and pinching a little at the shoulders. The trousers cling to a disproportionately powerful lower torso—a soccer player in long pants. His pointed white shoes are in need of repair; his white shirt is worn with the top buttons open. Something of the wastrel, something of the mobster, something too of the overprivileged boy. Where the woman's English is heavily accented, Sisovsky's is only mildly flawed, and articulated so confidently—with oddly elegant Oxonian vowels—that the occasional syntactical contusion strikes me as a form of cunning, an ironical game to remind his American host that he is, after all, only a refugee, little more than a newcomer to the tongue mastered already with so much fluency and charm. Beneath all this deference to me, I take him to be one of the strong ones, one of the stallions who has the strength of his outrage.

"Tell him to tell me about *his* book," I say to her. "What was it called?"

But on he continues about mine. "When we arrived in

Canada from Rome, yours was the first book that I bought. I have learned that it had a scandalous response here in America. When you were so kind to agree to see me, I went to the library to find out how Americans have perceived your work. The question interests me because of how Czechs perceived my own work, which also had a scandalous response."

"What was the scandal?"

"Please," he says, "I don't wish to compare our two books. Yours is a work of genius, and mine is nothing. When I studied Kafka, the fate of his books in the hands of the Kafkologists seemed to me to be more grotesque than the fate of Josef K. I feel this is true also with you. This scandalous response gives another grotesque dimension, and belongs now to your book as Kafkologine stupidities belong to Kafka. Even as the banning of my own little book creates a dimension not at all intended by me."

"Why was it banned, your book?"

"The weight of the stupidity you must carry is heavier than the weight of banning."

"Not true."

"I am afraid it is, *cher maître*. You come to belittle the meaning of your vocation. You come to believe that there is no literary culture that matters. There is a definite existential weakening of your position. This is regrettable because, in fact, you have written a masterpiece."

Yet he never says what it is about my book that he likes.

Maybe he doesn't really like it. Maybe he hasn't read it. Much subtlety in such persistence. The ruined exile will not be deflected from commiserating with the American success.

What's he want?

"But it's you," I remind him, "who's been denied the right to practice his profession. Whatever the scandal, I have been profusely—bizarrely—rewarded. Everything from an Upper East Side address to helping worthy murderers get out on parole. That's the power a scandal bestows over here. It's *you* who's been punished in the harshest way. Banning your book, prohibiting your publication, driving you from your country—what could be more burdensome and stupid than that? I'm glad you think well of my work, but don't be polite about *cher maître*'s situation, *mon cher ami*. What made what you wrote such a scandal?"

The woman says, "Zdenek, tell him."

"What is there to tell?" he says. "A satirical smile is harder for them than outright ideological fanaticism. I laughed. They are ideologues. I hate ideologues. That is what causes so much offense. It also causes my doubt."

I ask him to explain the doubt.

"I published one harmless little satire in Prague in 1967. The Russians came to visit in 1968 and I have not published anything since. There is nothing more to say. What interests me are these foolish reviews that I read in the library of your book. Not that they are foolish, that goes without saying. It is that there is not one which could be called intelligent. One reads such things in America and one is struck with terror for the future, for the world, for everything."

"Terror for the future, even for the world, I understand. But for 'everything'? Sympathize with a writer about his foolish reviews and you have a friend for life, Sisovsky, but now that this has been achieved, I'd like to hear about your doubt."

"Tell him about your *doubt*, Zdenek!"

"How can I? I don't even believe in my doubt, frankly. I don't think I have any doubt at all. But I think I should."

"Why?" I say.

"I remember the time before the invasion of Prague," he says. "I swear to you that every single review of your work could not have been published in Prague in the sixties—the level is too low. And this in spite of the fact that according to simplified notions we were a Stalinate country and the U.S.A. was the country of intellectual freedom."

"Zdenek, he wants to hear not about these reviews—he wishes to hear about your doubt!"

"Calm down," he tells her.

"The man is asking a question."

"I am answering it."

"Then do it. *Do it.* He has told you already that you have flattered him enough!" Italy, Canada, now New York—she is as sick of him as of their wandering. While he speaks her eyes momentarily close and she touches the distended vein in her temple—as though remembering yet

7

another irreversible loss. Sisovsky drinks my whiskey, she refuses even a cup of tea. She wants to go, probably all the way back to Czechoslovakia, and probably on her own.

I intervene—before she can scream—and ask him, "Could you have stayed on in Czechoslovakia, despite the banning of your book?"

"Yes. But if I had stayed in Czechoslovakia, I am afraid I would have taken the way of resignation. I could not write, speak in public, I could not even see my friends without being taken in for interrogation. To try to do something, anything, is to endanger one's own well-being, and the well-being of one's wife and children and parents. I have a wife there. I have a child and I have an aging mother who has already been deprived of enough. You choose resignation because you realize that there is nothing to be done. There is no resistance against the Russification of my country. The fact that the occupation is hated by everyone isn't any defense in the long run. You Americans think in terms of one year or two; Russians think in centuries. They know instinctively that they live in a long time, and that the time is theirs. They know it deeply, and they are right. The truth is that as time goes by, the population slowly accepts its fate. Eight years have passed. Only writers and intellectuals continue to be persecuted, only writing and thinking are suppressed; everybody else is content, content even with their hatred of the Russians, and mostly they live better than they ever have. Modesty alone demands that we leave them be. You can't keep clamoring about being published without wondering if it is only your vanity speaking. I am not a great genius like you. People have Musil and Proust and Mann and Nathan Zuckerman to read, why should they read me? My book was a scandal not only because of my satirical smile but because in 1967 when I was published I was twenty-five. The new generation. The future. But my generation of the future has made better peace with the Russians than anyone. For me to stay in Czechoslovakia and make trouble with the Russians about my little books —why? Why is another book from me important?"

"That isn't Solzhenitsyn's point of view."

"Good for him. Why should I pay everything to try to publish another book with a satirical smile? What am I proving by fighting against them and endangering myself and everyone I know? Unfortunately, however, as much as I mistrust the way of reckless vanity, I suspect even more the way of resignation. Not for others—they do as they must—but for myself. I am not a courageous person, but I cannot be out-and-out cowardly."

"Or is that also just vanity?"

"Exactly—I am *totally* in doubt. In Czechoslovakia, if I stay there, yes, I can find some kind of work and at least live in my own country and derive some strength from that. There I can at least be a Czech—but I cannot be a writer. While in the West, I can be a writer, but not a Czech. Here, where as a writer I am totally negligible, I am *only* a writer. As I no longer have all the other things that gave meaning to life—my country, my language, friends, family, memories, et cetera—here for me making literature is everything. But the only literature I can make is so much about life there that only there can it have the effect I desire."

"So, what's even heavier than the weight of the banning is this doubt that it foments."

"In me. Only in me. Eva has no doubt. She has only hatred."

Eva is astonished. "Hatred for what?"

"For everyone who has betrayed you," he says to her. "For everyone who deserted you. You hate them and wish they were dead."

"I don't even think of them anymore."

"You wish them to be tortured in Hell."

"I have forgotten them completely."

"I should like to tell you about Eva Kalinova," he says to me. "It is too vulgar to announce such a thing, but it is too ridiculous for you not to know. It is personally humiliating that I should ask you to endure the great drama of my doubt while Eva sits here like no one."

"I am happy to be sitting like no one," she says. "This is not necessary."

"Eva," he says, "is Prague's great Chekhovian actress. Go to Prague and ask. No one there will dispute it, not even the regime. There is no Nina since hers, no Irina, no Masha."

"I don't want this," she says.

"When Eva gets on the streetcar in Prague, people still applaud. All of Prague has been in love with her since she was eighteen."

"Is that why they write on my wall 'the Jew's whore'? Because they are in love with me? Don't be stupid. That is over."

"Soon she will be acting again," he assures me.

"To be an actress in America, you must speak English that does not give people a headache!"

"Eva, sit down."

But her career is finished. She cannot sit.

"You cannot be on the stage and speak English that nobody can understand! Nobody will hire you to do that. I do not want to perform in more plays—I have had enough of being an artificial person. I am tired of imitating all the touching Irinas and Ninas and Mashas and Sashas. It confuses me and it confuses everyone else. We are people who fantasize too much to begin with. We read too much, we feel too much, we fantasize too much —we want all the wrong things! I am *glad* to be finished with all my successes. The success comes to the person anyway, not to the acting. What good does it do? What does it serve? Only egomania. Brezhnev has given me a chance to be an ordinary nobody who performs a real job. I sell dresses—and dresses are needed more by people than stupid touching Chekhovian actresses!"

"But what," I ask, "do Chekhovian actresses need?"

"To be in the life of others the way they are in a play,

and not in a play the way they are supposed to be in the life of others! They need to be rid of their selfishness and their feelings and their looks and their art!" Beginning to cry, she says, "At last I am rid of mine!"

"Eva, tell him about your Jewish demons. He is the American authority on Jewish demons. She is pursued, Mr. Zuckerman, by Jewish demons. Eva, you must tell him about the Vice-Minister of Culture and what happened with him after you left your husband. Eva was married to somebody that in America you have never heard of, but in Czechoslovakia the whole country loves him. He is a very beloved theatrical personality. You can watch him on television every week. He has all the old mothers crying when he sings Moravian folk songs. When he talks to them with that dreadful voice, the girls are all swooning. You hear him on the jukeboxes, you hear him on the radio, wherever you go you hear this dreadful voice that is supposed to be a hot-blooded gypsy. If you are that man's wife you don't have to worry. You can play all the great heroines at the National Theater. You can have plenty of room to live. You can take all the trips you want abroad. If you are that man's wife, they leave you alone."

"He leaves you alone too," she says. "Zdenek, why do you persecute me? I do not care to be an ironical Czech character in an ironical Czech story. Everything that happens in Czechoslovakia, they shrug their shoulders and say, 'Pure Schweik, pure Kafka.' I am sick of them both."

"Tell me about your Jewish demons," I say.

"I don't have them," she replies, looking furiously at Sisovsky.

"Eva fell in love with a Mr. Polak and left her husband for him. Now, if you are Mr. Polak's mistress," Sisovsky says, "they do not leave you alone. Mr. Polak has had many mistresses and they have never left any of them alone. Eva Kalinova is married to a Czechoslovak Artist of Merit, but she leaves him to take up with a Zionist agent and bourgeois enemy of the people. And this is why they write 'the Jew's whore' on the wall outside the theater, and send poems to her in the mail about her immorality, and drawings of Polak with a big Jewish nose. This is why they write letters to the Minister of Culture denouncing her and demanding that she be removed from the stage. This is why she is called in to see the Vice-Minister of Culture. Leaving a great Artist of Merit and a boring, sentimental egomaniac like Petr Kalina for a Jew and a parasite like Pavel Polak, she is no better than a Jew herself."

"Please," says Eva, "stop telling this story. All these people, they suffer for their ideas and for their banned books, and for democracy to return to Czechoslovakia—they suffer for their principles, for their humanity, for their hatred of the Russians, and in this terrible story I am still suffering for love!"

" 'Do you know,' he says to her, our enlightened Vice-Minister of Culture, 'do you know, Madam Kalinova,' " Sisovsky continues, " 'that half our countrymen believe you

really are a Jewess, by blood?' Eva says to him, very dryly
—for Eva can be a very dry, very beautiful, very intelligent
woman when she is not angry with people or frightened
out of her wits—very dryly she says, 'My dear Mr. Vice-
Minister, my family was being persecuted as Protestants in
Bohemia in the sixteenth century.' But this does not stop
him—he knows this already. He says to her, 'Tell me—why
did you play the role of the Jewess Anne Frank on the
stage when you were only nineteen years old?' Eva an-
swers, 'I played the role because I was chosen from ten
young actresses. And all of them wanted it more than
the world.' 'Young actresses,' he asks her, 'or young
Jewesses?' "

"I beg you, Zdenek, I cannot hear my ridiculous story!
I cannot hear *your* ridiculous story! I am sick and tired
of hearing our story, I am sick and tired of *having* our
story! That was Europe, this is America! I shudder to
think I was ever that woman!"

" 'Young actresses,' he asks her, 'or young Jewesses?'
Eva says, 'What difference does that make? Some were
Jewish, I suppose. But I am not.' 'Well then,' he says to
Eva, 'why did you want to continue playing this Jewess
on the stage for two years, if you weren't, at the least, a
Zionist sympathizer even then?' Eva replies, 'I have played
a Jewess in *Ivanov* by Anton Chekhov. I have played a
Jewess in *The Merchant of Venice* by Shakespeare.' This
convinces him of nothing. That Eva had wanted to play
a Jewess even in a play by Anton Chekhov, where you

have to look for one high and low, does not, in the opinion of the vice-minister, strengthen her position. 'But everybody understands,' Eva explains to him, '. . . these are only *roles*. If half the country thinks I'm a Jew, that does not make it so. They once said I was part gypsy too; probably there are as many people who still believe that because of the ridiculous film I made with Petr. But, Mr. Vice-Minister,' Eva says, 'what everybody knows, what is true and indisputable, is that I am none of these things: *I am an actress.*' He corrects her. 'An actress, Madam Kalinova, who likes to portray Jewesses, who portrays them masterfully—*that* is what everyone knows. What everyone knows is that no one in all of our country can portray a Jewess better.' 'And if that is even true? Is that also a crime in this country now?' By then Eva is shouting and, of course, she is crying. She is shaking all over. And this makes him nice to her suddenly, certainly nicer than before. He offers brandy to calm her down. He explains that he is not talking about what is the law. He is not even speaking for himself. His heart happens to have been greatly moved in 1956 when he saw Eva playing little Anne Frank. He wept at her performance—he has never forgotten it. His confession causes Eva to become completely crazy. 'Then what are you talking about?' she asks him. 'The feelings of the people,' he replies. 'The sentiments of the great Czech people. To desert Petr Kalina, an Artist of Merit, to become the mistress of the Zionist Polak would have been damaging enough, but to the people it is unforgivable because of your long history of always playing Jewesses on the stage.' 'This makes no sense,' Eva tells him. 'It cannot be. The Czech people loved Anne Frank, they loved *me* for portraying her!' Here he removes from his file all these fake letters by all the offended members of the theatergoing public—fake, just like the writing on the theater walls. This closes the case. Eva is dismissed from the National Theater. The vice-minister is so pleased with himself that he goes around boasting how he handled Polak's whore and made that arrogant Jew bastard know just who is running this country. He believes that when the news reaches Moscow, the Russians will give him a medal for his cruelty and his anti-Semitism. They have a gold medal just for this. But instead he loses his job. The last I heard he was assistant editor of the publishing house of religious literature. Because the Czechs *did* love Anne Frank—and because somebody high up wants to be rid of the stupid vice-minister anyway—he is fired for how he has handled Eva Kalinova. Of course for Eva it would have been better if instead of firing the vice-minister they would restore her position as leading actress with the National Theater. But our system of justice is not yet so developed. It is stronger on punishment than on restitution."

"They are strong on *nothing*," says Eva. "It is that I am so weak. That I am stupid and cannot defend myself against all of these bullies! I cry, I shake, I cave in. I *deserve* what they do. In this world, still to carry on about a man! They should have cut my head off. *That* would have been justice!"

"And now," says Sisovsky, "she is with another Jew. At her age. Now Eva is ruined completely."

She erupts in Czech, he replies in English. "On Sunday," he says to her, "what will you do at home? Have a drink, Eviczka. Have some whiskey. Try to enjoy life."

Again, in Czech, she pleads with him, or berates him, or berates herself. In English, and again most gently, he says, "I understand. But *Zuckerman* is interested."

"I am going!" she tells me—"I must go!" and rushes from the living room.

"Well, I stay . . ." he mutters and empties his glass. Before I can get up to show her out, the door to my apartment is opened and slammed shut.

"Since you are curious," says Sisovsky, while I pour him another drink, "she said that she is going home and I said what will you do at home and she said, 'I am sick of your mind and I am sick of my body and I am sick to death of these boring stories!' "

"She wants to hear a new story."

"What she wants is to hear a new man. Today she is angry because she says I bring her here with me only to show her to you. What am I to do—leave her alone in our room to hang herself? On a Sunday? Wherever we go now in New York and there is a man, she accuses me of this. 'What is the function of this man?' she says. There are dramatic scenes where she calls me a pimp. I am the pimp because she wants to leave me and is afraid to leave me because in New York she is nobody and alone."

"And she can't go back to Prague?"

"It is better for her not to be Eva Kalinova here than not to be Eva Kalinova there. In Prague, Eva would go out of her mind when she saw who they had cast to play Madam Arkadina."

"But here she's out of her mind selling dresses."

"No," he says. "The problem is not dresses. It's Sundays. Sunday is not the best day in the émigré's week."

"Why did they let the two of you go?"

"The latest thing is to let people go, people who want to leave the country. Those who don't want to leave, they must keep silent. And those who don't want to leave, and who don't wish to keep silent, they finish up in jail."

"I didn't realize, Sisovsky, that on top of everything else you were Jewish."

"I resemble my mother, who was not. My father was the Jew. Not only a Jew, but like you, a Jew writing about Jews; like you, Semite-obsessed all his life. He wrote hundreds of stories about Jews, only he did not publish one. My father was an introverted man. He taught mathematics in the high school in our provincial town. The writing was for himself. Do you know Yiddish?"

"I am a Jew whose language is English."

"My father's stories were in Yiddish. To read the stories, I taught myself Yiddish. I cannot speak. I never had him to speak it to. He died in 1941. Before the Jews began even to be deported, a Nazi came to our house and shot him."

"Why him?"

"Since Eva is no longer here, I can tell you. It's another of my boring European stories. One of her favorites. In our town there was a Gestapo officer who loved to play chess. After the occupation began, he found out that my father was the chess master of the region, and so he had him to his house every night. My father was horribly shy of people, even of his students. But because he believed that my mother and my brother would be protected if he was courteous with the officer, he went whenever he was called. And they *were* protected. All the Jews in the town were huddled into the Jewish quarter. For the others things got a little worse every day, but not for my family. For more than a year nobody bothered them. My father could no longer teach at the high school, but he was now allowed to go around as a private tutor to earn some money. At night, after our dinner, he would leave the Jewish quarter and go to play chess with the Gestapo officer. Well, stationed in the town there was another Gestapo officer. He had a Jewish dentist whom *he* was protecting. The dentist was fixing all his teeth for him. His family too was left alone, and the dentist was allowed to continue with his practice. One Sunday, a Sunday probably much like today, the two Gestapo officers went out drinking together and they got drunk, much the way, thanks to your hospitality, we are getting nicely drunk here. They had an argument. They were good friends, so it must have been a terrible argument, because the one who played chess with my father was so angry that he walked over to the dentist's house and got the dentist out of bed and shot him. This enraged the other Nazi so much that the next morning he came to our house and he shot my father, and my brother also, who was eight. When he was taken before the German commandant, my father's murderer explained, 'He shot my Jew, so I shot his.' 'But why did you shoot the child?' 'That's how God-damn angry I was, sir.' They were reprimanded and told not to do it again. That was all. But even that reprimand was something. There was no law in those days against shooting Jews in their houses, or even on the street."

"And your mother?"

"My mother hid on a farm. There I was born, two months later. Neither of us looks like my father. Neither did my brother, but his short life was just bad luck. We two survived."

"And why did your father, with an Aryan wife, write stories in Yiddish? Why not in Czech? He must have spoken Czech to the students at the high school."

"Czech was for Czechs to write. He married my mother, but he never thought he was a real Czech. A Jew who marries a Jew is able at home to forget he's a Jew. A Jew who marries an Aryan like my mother has her face there always to remind him."

"He didn't ever write in German?"

"We were not Sudeten Germans, you see, and we were not Prague Jews. Of course German was less foreign to him than Czech, because of Yiddish. German he insisted on for my brother to be properly educated. He himself read Lessing, Herder, Goethe, and Schiller, but his own father had been, not even a town Jew like him, he had been a Jew in the farmlands, a village shopkeeper. To the Czechs such Jews spoke Czech, but in the family they spoke only Yiddish. All of this is in my father's stories: homelessness beyond homelessness. One story is called 'Mother Tongue.' Three pages only, about a little Jewish boy who speaks bookish German, Czech without the native flavor, and the Yiddish of people simpler than himself. Kafka's homelessness, if I may say so, was nothing beside my father's. Kafka had at least the nineteenth century in his blood—all those Prague Jews did. Kafka belonged to literature, if nothing else. My father belonged to nothing. If he had lived, I think that I would have developed a great antagonism to my father. I would have thought, 'What is this man so lonely for? Why is he so sad and withdrawn? He should join the revolution—then he would not sit with his head in his hands, wondering where he belongs.'"

"Sons are famous the world over for generous thoughts about fathers."

"When I came to New York and wrote my letter to you, I said to Eva, 'I am a relative of this great man.' I was thinking of my father and his stories. Since we have come from Europe, I have already read fifty American novels about Jews. In Prague I knew nothing about this incredible phenomenon and how vast it was. Between the wars in Czechoslovakia my father was a freak. Even had he wished to publish his stories, where would they have appeared? Even if he had published all two hundred of them, no one would have paid attention—not to that subject. But in America my father would have been a celebrated writer. Had he emigrated before I was born, had he come to New York City in his thirties, he would have been discovered by some helpful person and published in the best magazines. He would be something more now than just another murdered Jew. For years I never thought of my father, now every minute I wonder what he would make of the America I am seeing. I wonder what America would have made of him. He would be seventy-two. I am obsessed now with this great Jewish writer that might have been."

"His stories are that good?"

"I am not exaggerating his excellence. He was a deep and wonderful writer."

"Like whom? Sholem Aleichem? Isaac Babel?"

"I can tell you only that he was elliptical, humble, self-conscious, all in his own way. He could be passionate, he could be florid, he could be erudite—he could be anything. No, this is not the Yiddish of Sholem Aleichem. This is the Yiddish of Flaubert. His last work, ten little stories about Nazis and Jews, the saddest commentary I have ever read about the worst life has to offer. They are about the family of the Nazi commandant he played chess with at night. About his visits to the house and how charmed they all were. He called them 'Stories about Chess.' "

"What became of those stories?"

"They are with my books in Prague. And my books in Prague are with my wife. And my wife does not like me so much anymore. She has become a drunk because of me. Our daughter has become crazy because of me and lives with her aunt because of me. The police will not leave my wife alone because of me. I don't think I'll ever see my father's stories again. My mother goes to ask my wife for her husband's stories and my wife recounts for her all of my infidelities. She shows my mother photographs of all my mistresses, unclothed. These too I unfortunately left behind with my books."

"Will she destroy your father's stories?"

"No, no. She couldn't do it. Olga is a writer too. In Czechoslovakia she is very well known for her writing, for her drinking, and for showing everybody her cunt. You would like Olga. She was once very beautiful, with beautiful long legs and gray cat-eyes and her books were once beautiful too. She is a most compliant woman. It is I alone whom she opposes. Anything another man wants, Olga will do it. She will do it well. If you were to visit Prague, and you were to meet Olga and Olga were to fall in love with you, she would even give you my father's stories, if you were to go about it the right way. She loves love. She does anything for love. An American writer, a famous, attractive, American genius who does not practice the American innocence to a shameless degree—if he were to ask for my father's stories, Olga would give them to him, I am sure of it. The only thing is not to lay her too soon."

Prague, Feb. 4, 1976

At Klenek's every Tuesday night, with or without Klenek in residence, there is a wonderful party to go to. Klenek is currently directing a film in France. Because he is technically still married to a German baroness, he is by Czech law allowed to leave the country half of each year, ostensibly to be with her. The Czech film industry is no longer open to him, but he continues to live in his palazzo and is permitted to associate with his old friends, many of whom the regime now honors as its leading enemies. No one is sure why he is privileged—perhaps because Klenek is useful propaganda, somebody the regime can hold up to its foreign critics as an artist who lives as he wishes. Also, by letting him work abroad, they can continue to tax his large foreign earnings. And, explains Bolotka, Klenek may well be a spy. "Probably he tells them things," says Bolotka. "Not that it matters. Nobody tells him anything, and he knows nobody tells him anything, and they know nobody tells him anything."

"What's the point then?"

"With Klenek the point is to spy not on politics but on sex. The house is bugged everywhere. The secret police listen to the tape recordings of Klenek's parties. They prowl outside and look in the windows. It's their job. Sometimes they even see something and get excited. This is a pleasant distraction from the pettiness and viciousness of their regular work. It does them good. It does everybody good. Fifteen-year-old girls come to Klenek's. They dress up like streetwalkers and come from as far away as a hundred miles. Everybody, even schoolchildren, is looking for fun. You like orgies, you come with me. Since the Russians, the best orgies in Europe are in Czechoslovakia. Less liberty, better fucks. You can do whatever you want at Klenek's. No drugs, but plenty of whiskey. You can fuck, you can masturbate, you can look at dirty pictures, you can look at yourself in the mirror, you can do nothing. All the best people are there. Also the worst. We are all comrades now. Come to the orgy, Zuckerman—you will see the final stage of the revolution."

Klenek's is a small seventeenth-century palazzo on the Kampa, a little residential island we reach by descending a long wet stairway from the Charles Bridge. Standing in the cobbled square outside of Klenek's, I hear the Vltava churning past the deep stone embankment. I've walked with Bolotka from my hotel through the maze of the ghetto, passing on the way the capsized tombstones of what he informs me is the oldest Jewish cemetery left in Europe. Within the iron grating, the jumble of crooked, eroded markers looks less like a place of eternal rest than something a cyclone has torn apart. Twelve thousand Jews buried in layers in what in New York would be a small parking lot. Drizzle dampening the tombstones, ravens in the trees.

Klenek's: large older women in dark rayon raincoats, young pretty women with jewels and long dresses, stout middle-aged men dressed in boxy suits and looking like postal clerks, elderly men with white hair, a few slight young men in American jeans—but no fifteen-year-old girls. Bolotka may be having some fun exaggerating for his visitor the depths of Prague depravity—a little cold water on free-world fantasies of virtuous political suffering.

Beside me on a sofa, Bolotka explains who is who and who likes what.

"That one was a journalist till they fired him. He loves pornography. I saw him with my eyes fucking a girl from behind and reading a dirty book at the same time. That one, he is a terrible abstract painter. The best abstract painting he did was the day the Russians came. He went out and painted over all the street signs so the tanks wouldn't know where they were. He has the longest prick in Prague. That one, the little clerk, that is Mr. Vodicka.

He is a very good writer, an excellent writer, but everything scares him. If he sees a petition, he passes out. When you bring him to life again, he says he will sign it: he has ninety-eight percent reason to sign, and only two percent reason not to sign, and he has only to think about the two percent and he will sign. By the next day the two percent has grown to one hundred percent. Just this week Mr. Vodicka told the government that if he made bad politics he is sorry. He is hoping this way they will let him write again about his perversion."

"Will they?"

"Of course not. They will tell him now to write a historical novel about Pilsen beer."

We are joined by a tall, slender woman, distinguished by a mass of hair dyed the color of a new penny and twisted down over her forehead in curls. Heavy white makeup encases her sharp, birdlike face. Her eyes are gray cat-eyes, her smile is beckoning. "I know who you are," she whispers to me.

"And you are who?"

"I don't know. I don't even feel I exist." To Bolotka: "Do I exist?"

"This one is Olga," Bolotka says. "She has the best legs in Prague. She is showing them to you. Otherwise she does not exist."

Mr. Vodicka approaches Olga, bows like a courtier, and takes her hand. He is a little, unobtrusive man of sixty, neatly dressed and wearing heavy spectacles. Olga pays him no attention.

"My lover wants to kill me," she says to me.

Mr. Vodicka is whispering in her ear. She waves him away, but passionately he presses her hand to his cheek.

"He wants to know if she has any boys for him," Bolotka explains.

"Who is she?"

"She was the most famous woman in the country. Olga wrote our love stories. A man stood her up in a restaurant and she wrote a love story, and the whole country talked about why he stood her up. She had an abortion and she told the doctor it could be one of eleven men, and the whole country debated whether it could actually be so many. She went to bed with a woman and the whole country read the story and was guessing who it was. She was seventeen, she already wrote a bestseller, *Touha*. Longing. Our Olga loves most the absent thing. She loves the Bohemian countryside. She loves her childhood. But always something is missing. Olga suffers the madness that follows after loss. And this even *before* the Russians. Klenek saw her in a café, a tall country girl, her heart full of *touha*, and he took her here to live with him. This is over twenty years ago. For seven years Olga was married. She had a child. Poor child. Now her husband runs off with the other famous woman in our country, a beautiful Czech actress who he will destroy in America, and Olga, Klenek looks after."

"Why does she need looking after?"

"Why do you need looking after?" Bolotka asks her.

"This is awful," she says. "I hear stories about myself tonight. Stories about who I fuck. I would never fuck such people."

"Why do you need looking after, Olga?" Bolotka asks again.

"Because I'm shaking. Feel me shaking. I never stop shaking. I am frightened of everything." Points to me. "I am frightened of him." She flops down onto the sofa, in the space between Bolotka and me. I feel pressing against mine the best legs in Prague. Also believe I feel the *touha*.

"You don't act frightened," I say.

"Since I am frightened of everything it is as well to go in one direction as the other. If I get into too much trouble, you will come and marry me and take me to America. I will telegram and you will come and save me." She says to Bolotka, "Do you know what Mr. Vodicka wants now? He has a boy who has never seen a woman. He wants me to show it to him. He is going into the street to get him." Then, to me: "Why are you in Prague? Are you looking for Kafka? The intellectuals all come here looking for Kafka. Kafka is dead. They should be looking for Olga. Are you planning to make love to anybody in Prague? If so, you will let me know." To Bolotka: "Kouba. There is Kouba! I cannot be in this house with that Kouba!" To me: "You want to know why I need looking after? *Because of stupid communists like Kouba!*" She points to a short man with a bald head who is animatedly entertaining a circle of friends in the center of the milling crowd. "Kouba knew what the good life was for all of us. It has taken the Koubas twenty years to learn, and they're *still* too stupid to learn. All brains and no intelligence. *None.* Kouba is one of our great communist heroes. It is surprising he is still in Prague. Not all of our great communist heroes who were in Italy with their girl friends when the Russians invaded have bothered to come back from their holiday yet. Do you know why? Because when the Russians occupied Prague, at last they were free of their wives. Some of our greatest communist heroes are now with their girl friends teaching Marxism-Leninism in New York. They are only sorry that the revolution fell into the wrong hands. Otherwise they are like Kouba—still one hundred percent sure they are right. So why do you come to Prague? You are not looking for Kafka, none of our heroes in New York sent you, and you don't want to fuck. I love this word fuck. Why don't we have this word, Rudolf?" To me again: "Teach me how to say fuck. This is a good fucking party. I was really fucked. Wonderful word. Teach me."

"Shut the fuck up."

"Beautiful word. Shut the fuck up. More."

"Fuck it all. Fuck everything."

"Yes, fuck it all. Fuck everything and fuck everybody. Fuck the world till it cannot fuck me anymore. See, I learn fast. In America I would be a famous writer like you. You are afraid to fuck me. Why is that? Why do you write this book about fucking that makes you so famous if you are afraid to fuck somebody? You hate fucking everybody or just me?"

"Everybody."

"He is kind to you, Olga," Bolotka says. "He is a gentleman, so he doesn't tell you the truth because you are so hopeless."

"Why am I hopeless?"

"Because in America the girls don't talk to him like this."

"What do they say in America? Teach me to be an American girl."

"First you would take your hand off my prick."

"I see. Okay. Now what?"

"We would talk to each other. We would try to get to know each other first."

"Why? I don't understand this. Talk about what? The Indians?"

"Yes, we would talk at length about the Indians."

"And *then* I put my hand on your prick."

"That's right."

"And then you fuck me."

"That would be the way we would do it, yes."

"It is a very strange country."

"It's one of them."

Mr. Vodicka, pink with excitement, is dragging the boy through the room. Everything excites Mr. Vodicka: Olga

dismissing him like a bothersome child, Bolotka address-
ing him like a whipped dog, the indifferent boy weary
already of being so cravenly desired. The stage-set splen-
dors of Klenek's drawing room—velvet burgundy draper-
ies, massive carved antiques, threadbare Oriental carpets,
tiers of dark romantic landscapes leaning from the paneled
oak walls—evoke no more from the boy than a mean little
smirk. Been everywhere already, seen the best in brothels
by the time he was twelve.

Mr. Vodicka is fastidious with the introductions.
Bolotka translates. "He is saying to Olga that the boy has
never seen a woman. That's how Mr. Vodicka has got him
in from the street. He promised he would show him one.
He is telling Olga that she has to show it to him, otherwise the boy will go."

"What do you do now?" I ask Olga.

"What I do? I show it to him. I have you to fuck me.
Mr. Vodicka has only dreams to fuck. He is more frightened of everything than I am."

"You're doing it out of sentiment."

Placing my hands over her breasts, Olga says, "If it
weren't for sentiment, Zuckerman, one person would not
pass another person a glass of water."

Czech exchange. Bolotka translates.

Olga says to Mr. V., "First I want to see his."

The boy won't hear of it. Plump, smooth, dark, and
cruel: a very creamy caramel dessert.

Olga waves her hand. The hell with it, get out, go.

"Why do you want to see it?" I ask her.

"I don't. I have seen too many already. Mr. Vodicka wants to see it."

For five minutes she addresses the boy in the softest, most caressing Czech, until, at last, he shuffles childishly toward the sofa and, frowning at the ceiling, undoes his zipper. Olga summons him one step closer and then, with two fingers and a thumb, reaches delicately into his trousers. The boy yawns. She withdraws his penis. Mr. Vodicka looks. We all look. Light entertainment in occupied Prague.

"Now," says Olga, "they will put on television a photograph of me with his prick. Everywhere in this house there are cameras. On the street someone is always snapping my picture. Half the country is employed spying on the other half. I am a rotten degenerate bourgeois negativist pseudoartist—and this will prove it. This is how they destroy me."

"Why do you do it then?"

"It is too silly not to." In English she says to Mr. V., "Come, I'll show it to him." She zips the boy up and leads him away, Mr. Vodicka eagerly following.

"*Are* cameras hidden here?" I ask Bolotka.

"Klenek says no, only microphones. Maybe there are cameras in the bedrooms, for the fucking. But you go on the floor and turn the light out. Don't worry. Don't be scared. You want to fuck her, fuck her on the floor. Nobody would take your picture there."

"Who is the lover who wants to kill her?"

"Don't be afraid of him; he won't kill her or you either. He doesn't even want to see her. One night Olga is drunk and angry because he is tired of her, and she finds out he has a new girl friend, so she telephones the police and she tells them that he has threatened to murder her. The police come, and by then the joke is over and he is undressed and sorry about the new girl friend. But the police are also drunk, so they take him away. The whole country is drunk. Our president must go on television for three hours to tell the people to stop drinking and go back to work. You get onto a streetcar at night when the great working class is on its way home, and the great working class smells like a brewery."

"What happened to Olga's lover?"

"He has a note from a doctor saying he is a psychiatric case."

"Is he?"

"He carries the note to be left alone. They leave you alone if you can prove you are crazy. He is a perfectly reasonable person: he is interested in fucking women and writing poems, and not in stupid politics. This proves he is *not* crazy. But the police come and they read the note and they take him to the lunatic asylum. He is still there. Olga thinks now he will kill her because of what she did. But he is happy where he is. In the lunatic asylum he is not required to be a worker all day in the railway office. There he has some peace and quiet and at last he writes something again. There he has the whole day to write poems instead of railroad tickets."

"How do you all live like this?"

"Human adaptability is a great blessing."

Olga, who has returned, sits herself on my lap.

"Where is Mr. Vodicka?" I ask her.

"He stays in the loo with the boy."

"What did you do to them, Olga?" Bolotka asks.

"I did nothing. When I showed it to him, the boy screamed. I took down my pants and he screamed, 'It's awful.' But Mr. Vodicka was bending over, with his hands on his knees, and studying me through his thick glasses. Maybe he wants to write about something new. He is studying me through his glasses, and then he says to the boy, 'Oh, I don't know, my friend—it's not our cup of tea, but from an aesthetic point of view it's not *horrible*.'"

Ten-thirty. I am to meet Hos and Hoffman in a wine bar at eleven. Everyone believes I am visiting Prague to commiserate with their proscribed writers when in fact I am here to strike a deal with the woman full of *touha* on my lap.

"You have to get up, Olga. I'm going."

"I come with you."

"You must have patience," Bolotka says to me. "Ours is a small country. We do not have so many millions of fifteen-year-old girls. But if you will have patience, she will come. And she will be worth it. The little Czech dumpling that we all like to eat. What is your hurry? What are you afraid of? You see—nothing happens. You do whatever you want in Prague and nobody cares. You cannot have such freedom in New York."

"He does not want a girl of fifteen," says Olga. "They are old whores by now, those little girls. He wants one who is forty."

I slide Olga off my lap and stand up to leave.

"Why do you act like this?" Olga asks. "You come all the way to Czechoslovakia and then you act like this. I will never see you again."

"Yes you will."

"You are lying. You will go back to those American girls and talk about Indians and fuck them. Next time you will tell me before, and I will study my Indian tribes and then we will fuck."

"Have lunch with me tomorrow, Olga. I'll pick you up here."

"But what about *tonight*? Why don't you fuck me *now*? Why are you leaving me, if you like me? I don't understand these American writers."

Neither, if they could see me, would my American readers. I am not fucking everyone, or indeed anyone, but sit quietly on the sofa being polite. I am a dignified, well-behaved, reliable spectator, secure, urbane, calm, polite, the quiet respectable one who does not take his trousers off, and *these* are the menacing writers. All the treats and blandishments, all the spoils that spoil are mine, and yet

36

what a witty, stylish comedy of manners these have-nots of Prague make out of their unbearable condition, this crushing business of being completely balked and walking the treadmill of humiliation. They, silenced, are all mouth. I am only ears—and plans, an American gentleman abroad, with the bracing if old-fashioned illusion that he is playing a worthwhile, dignified, and honorable role.

Bolotka offers Olga a comforting explanation for why she is no longer in my lap. "He is a middle-class boy. Leave him alone."

"But this is a classless society," she says. "This is socialism. What good is socialism if when I want to nobody will fuck me? All the great international figures come to Prague to see our oppression, but none of them will ever fuck me. Why is that? Sartre was here and he would not fuck me. Simone de Beauvoir came with him and she would not fuck me. Heinrich Böll, Carlos Fuentes, Graham Greene—and none of them will fuck me. Now you, and it is the same thing. You think to sign a petition will save Czechoslovakia, *but what will save Czechoslovakia would be to fuck Olga.*"

"Olga is drunk," Bolotka says.

"She's also crying," I point out.

"Don't worry about her," Bolotka says. "This is just Olga."

"Now," says Olga, "they will interrogate me about you. For six hours they will interrogate me about you, and I won't even be able to tell them we fucked."

"Is that what happens?" I ask Bolotka.

"Their interrogations are not to be dramatized," he says. "It is routine work. Whenever someone is questioned by Czech police he is questioned about everything that he can be asked. They are interested in everything. Now they are interested in you, but it does not mean that to be in touch with you could compromise anybody and that the police could accuse people who are in touch with you. They don't need that to accuse people. If they want to accuse you, they accuse you, and they don't need anything. If they interrogate me about why you came to Czechoslovakia, I will tell them."

"Yes? What will you say?"

"I will tell them you came for the fifteen-year-old girls. I will say, 'Read his book and you will see why he came.' Olga will be all right. In a couple of weeks Klenek returns home and Olga will be fine. You don't have to bother to fuck her tonight. Someone will do it, don't worry."

"I will *not* be all right," Olga cries. "Marry me and take me away from here. Zuckerman, if you marry me, they must let me go. That is the law—even *they* obey it. You wouldn't have to fuck me. You could fuck the American girls. You wouldn't have to love me, or even give me money."

"And she would scrub your floors," says Bolotka, "and iron your beautiful shirts. Wouldn't you, Olga?"

"Yes! Yes! I would iron your shirts all day long."

"That would be the first week," Bolotka says. "Then

would begin the second week and the excitement of being Mr. Olga."

"That isn't true," she says, "I would leave him alone."

"Then would begin the vodka," Bolotka says. "Then would begin the adventures."

"Not in America," weeps Olga.

"Oh," says Bolotka, "you would not be homesick for Prague in New York City?"

"No!"

"Olga, in America you would shoot yourself."

"I will shoot myself *here*!"

"With what?" asks Bolotka.

"A tank! Tonight! I will steal a Russian tank and I will shoot myself with it tonight!"

Bolotka occupies a dank room at the top of a bleak stairwell on a street of tenements near the outskirts of Prague. I visited him there earlier in the day. He reassures me, when he observes me looking sadly around, that I shouldn't feel too bad about his standard of living—this was his hideaway from his wife long before his theater was disbanded and he was forbidden to produce his "decadent" revues. For a man of his predilections it really is the *best* place to live. "It excites young girls," Bolotka informs me, "to be fucked in squalor." He is intrigued by my herringbone tweed suit and asks to try it on to see how it feels to be a rich American writer. He is a stoop-shouldered man, large and shambling, with a wide Mongol face, badly pitted skin, and razor-blade eyes, eyes like rifts in the bone of his skull, slitted green eyes whose manifesto is "You will jam nothing bogus into this brain." He has a wife somewhere, even children; recently the wife's arm was broken when she tried to prevent the police from entering their apartment to impound her absentee husband's several thousand books.

"Why does she care so much about you?"

"She doesn't—she hates me. But she hates them more. Old married couples in Prague have something to hate now even more than each other."

A month earlier the police came to the door of Bolotka's hole at the top of the stairwell to inform him that the country's leading troublemakers were being given papers to leave. They would allow him forty-eight hours to get out.

"I said to them, 'Why don't *you* leave? That would amount to the same thing, you know. I give *you* forty-eight hours.'"

But would he *not* be better off in Paris, or across the border in Vienna, where he has a reputation as a theatrical innovator and could resume his career?

"I have sixteen girl friends in Prague," he replies. "How can I leave?"

I am handed his robe to keep myself warm while he undresses and gets into my suit. "You look even more like a gorilla," I say, when he stands to model himself in my clothes.

"And even in my disgraceful dressing gown," he says, "you look like a happy, healthy, carefree impostor."

Bolotka's story.

"I was nineteen years old, I was a student at the university. I wanted like my father to be a lawyer. But after one year I decide I must quit and enroll at the School of Fine Arts. Of course I have first to go for an interview. This is 1950. Probably I would have to go to fifty interviews, but I only got to number one. I went in and they took out my 'record.' It was a foot thick. I said to them, 'How can it be a foot thick, I haven't lived yet. I have had no life—how can you have all this information?' But they don't explain. I sit there and they look it over and they say I cannot quit. The workers' money is being spent on my education. The workers have invested a year in my future as a lawyer. The workers have not made this investment so I can change my mind and decide to become a fine artist. They tell me that I cannot matriculate at the School of Fine Arts, or anywhere ever again, and so I said okay and went home. I didn't care that much. It wasn't so bad. I didn't have to become a lawyer, I had some girl friends, I had my prick, I had books, and to talk to and to keep me company, I had my childhood friend Blecha. Only they had him to talk with too. Blecha was planning then to be a famous poet and a famous novelist and a famous playwright. One night he got drunk and he admitted to me that he was spying on me. They knew he was an old friend and they knew that he wrote, and they knew he came to see me, so they hired him to spy on me and to write a report once a week. But he was a terrible writer. He is still a terrible writer. They told him that when they read his reports they could make no sense of them. They told him everything he wrote about me is unbelievable. So I said, 'Blecha, don't be depressed, let me see the reports—probably they are not as bad as they say. What do they know?' But they *were* terrible. He missed the point of everything I said, he got everything backwards about when I went where, and the writing was a disgrace. Blecha was afraid they were going to fire him— he was afraid they might even suspect him of playing some kind of trick, out of loyalty to me. And if that went into *his* record, he would be damaged for the rest of his life. Besides, all the time he should be spending on his poems and his stories and his plays, he was spending listening to me. He was getting nothing accomplished for himself. He was full of sadness over this. He had thought he could just betray a few hours a day and otherwise get on with being National Artist, Artist of Merit, and winner of the State Award for Outstanding Work. Well, it was obvious what to do. I said, 'Blecha, I will follow myself for you. I know what I do all day better than you, and I have nothing else to keep me busy. I will spy on myself and I will write it up, and you can submit it to them as your own. They will wonder how your rotten writing has improved overnight, but you just tell them you were sick. This way you won't have anything damaging on your record, and I can be rid of your company, you shitface.' Blecha was thrilled. He gave me half of what they paid him and everything was fine—until they decided that he was such a good spy and such a good writer, they promoted him. He was terrified. He came to me and said I had gotten him into this and so I had to help him. They were putting him now to spy on bigger troublemakers than me. They were even using his reports in the Ministry of Interior to teach new recruits. He said, 'You have the knack of it, Rudolf, with you it's just a technique. I am too imaginative for this work. But if I say no to them now, it will go in my record and I will be damaged by it later on. I could be seriously damaged now, if they knew you had written the reports on yourself.' So this is how I made a bit of a living when I was young. I taught our celebrated Artist of Merit and winner of the State Award for Outstanding Work how to write in plain Czech and describe a little what life is like. It was not easy. The man could not describe a shoelace. He did not know the word for anything. And he saw nothing. I would say, 'But, Blecha, was the friend sad or happy, clumsy or graceful, did he smoke, did he listen mostly or did he talk? Blecha, how will you ever become a great writer if you are such a bad spy?' This made him angry with me. He did not like my insults. He said spying was sickening to him and caused him to have writer's block. He said he could not use his creative talent while his spirit was being compromised like this. For me it was different. Yes, he had to tell me—it was different for me because I did not have high artistic ideals. I did not have any ideals. If I did I would not agree to spy on myself. I certainly would not take money for it. He had come to lose his respect for me. This is a sad irony to him, because when I left university, it was my integrity that meant so much to him and our friendship. Blecha told me this again recently. He was having lunch with Mr. Knap, another of our celebrated Artists of Merit and winner of the State Award for Outstanding Work, and secretary now of their Writers' Union. Blecha was quite drunk and always when he is quite drunk Blecha gets over-emotional and must tell you the truth. He came up to the table where I was having my lunch and he asked if everything is all right. He said he wished he could help an old friend in trouble, and then he whispered, 'Perhaps in a few months' time . . . but they do not like that you are so alienated, Rudolf. The phenomenon of alienation is not approved of from above. Still, for you I will do all that I can . . .' But then he sat suddenly down at the table and he said, 'But you must not go around Prague telling lies about me, Rudolf. Nobody believes you anyway. My books are everywhere. Schoolchildren read my poems, tens of thousands of people read my novels, on TV they perform my plays. You only make yourself look irresponsible and bitter by telling that story. And, if I may say so, a little crazy.' So I said to him, 'But, Blecha, I don't tell it. I have never told it to a soul.' And he said, 'Come now, my dear old friend

—how then does everybody know?' And so I said, 'Because their children read your poems, they themselves
have read your novels, and when they turn on TV, they
see your plays.' "

Prague, Feb. 5, 1976

The phone awakens me at quarter to eight.

"This is your wife-to-be. Good morning. I am going to
visit you. I am in the lobby of the hotel. I am coming now
to visit you in your room."

"No, no. I'll come down to you. It was to be lunch, not
breakfast."

"Why are you scared for me to visit you when I love
you?" asks Olga.

"It's not the best idea here. You know that."

"I am coming up."

"You're going to get yourself in trouble."

"Not me," she says.

I'm still doing up my trousers when she is at the door,
wearing a long suede coat that might have seen her
through trench warfare, and a pair of tall leather boots
that look as if she'd been farming in them. Against the
worn, soiled animal skins, her white neck and white face
appear dramatically vulnerable—you can see why people do
things to her that she does not necessarily like: bedraggled,

bold, and helpless, a deep ineradicable sexual helplessness such as once made bourgeois husbands so proud in the drawing room and so confident in bed. *Since I am frightened of everything, it is as well to go in one direction as the other.* Well, not only is she going, she's gone: she is reckless desperation incarnate.

I let her in quickly and close the door. "Prudence isn't your strong point."

"This I have never heard. Why do you say this?" she asks.

I point to the brass chandelier suspended above the bed, a favored place, Sisovsky had already told me back in New York, for the installation of a bugging device. "In your room," he warned me, "be careful about what you say. There are devices hidden everywhere. And on the phone it is best to say nothing. Don't mention the manuscript to her on the phone."

She drops into a chair beside the window while I continue to dress.

"You must understand," she says loudly, "that I am not marrying you for your money. I am marrying you," she continues, gesturing toward the light fixture, "because you tell me you love me at first sight, and because I believe this, and because at first sight I love you."

"You haven't been to sleep."

"How can I sleep? I am thinking only of my love for you, and I am happy and sad all at once. When I am thinking of our marriage and our children I do not want to sleep."

"Let's have breakfast somewhere. Let's get out of here."

"First tell me you love me."

"I love you."

"Is this why you marry me? For love?"

"What other reason could there be?"

"Tell me what you love most about me."

"Your sense of reality."

"But you must not love me for my sense of reality, you must love me for myself. Tell me all the reasons you love me."

"At breakfast."

"No. Now. I cannot marry a man who I have only just met"—she is scribbling on a piece of paper as she speaks —"and risk my happiness by making the wrong choice. I must be sure. I owe it to myself. And to my aged parents."

She hands me the note and I read it. *You cannot trust Czech police to understand ANYTHING, even in Czech. You must speak CLEAR and SLOW and LOUD.*

"I love your wit," I say.

"My beauty?"

"I love your beauty."

"My flesh?"

"I love your flesh."

"You love when we make love?"

47

"Indescribably."

Olga points to the chandelier. "What means 'indescribably,' darling?"

"More than words can say."

"It is much better fucking than with the American girls."

"It's the best."

In the hotel elevator, as we ride down along with the uniformed operator (another police agent, according to Bolotka) and three Japanese early-risers, Olga asks, "*Do you fuck anybody yet in Czechoslovakia?*"

"No, Olga, I haven't. Though a few people in Czechoslovakia may yet fuck me."

"How much is a room at this hotel?"

"I don't know."

"Of course. You're so rich you don't have to know. Do you know why they bug these big hotels, and always above the bed?"

"Why?"

"They listen in the rooms to the foreigners fucking. They want to hear how the women are coming in the different languages. Zuckerman, how are they coming in America? Teach me which words the American girls say."

In the lobby, the front-desk clerk moves out from behind the reception counter and crosses the lobby to meet us. Politely excusing himself to me, he addresses Olga in Czech.

"Speak English!" she demands. "I want him to understand! I want him to hear this insult in English!"

A stocky gray-haired man with formal manners and a heavy unsmiling face, the clerk is oblivious to her rage; he continues unemotionally in Czech.

"What is it?" I ask her.

"Tell him!" she shouts at the clerk. "Tell him what you want!"

"Sir, the lady must show her identity card. It is a regulation."

"Why is it a regulation?" she demands. "Tell him!"

"Foreign guests must register with a passport. Czech citizens must show an identity card if they go up to the rooms to make a call."

"Except if the Czech is a prostitute! Then she does not have to show anything but money! Here—I am a prostitute. Here is your fifty kroner—leave us in peace!"

He turns away from the money she is sticking into his face.

To me Olga explains, "I am sorry, Mister, I should have told you. Whipping a woman is against the law in a civilized country, even if she is being paid to be beaten. But everything is all right if you pay off the scum. Here," she cries, turning again to the clerk, "here is a hundred! I do not mean to insult you! Here is a hundred and fifty!"

"I need an identity card for Madame, please."

"You know who I am," she snarls, "everybody in this country knows who I am."

"I must record the number in my ledger, Madame."

"Tell me, please, why do you embarrass me like this in front of my prospective husband? Why do you try to make me ashamed of my nationality in front of the man I love? Look at him! Look at how he dresses! Look at his coat with a velvet collar! On his trousers he has buttons and not a little zipper like you! Why do you try to give such a man second thoughts about marrying a Czech woman?"

"I wish only to see her identity card, sir. I will return it immediately."

"Olga," I say softly, "enough."

"Do you see?" she shouts at the clerk. "Now he is disgusted. And do you know why? Because he is thinking, Where are their fine old European manners? What kind of country permits such a breach of etiquette toward a lady in the lobby of a grand hotel?"

"Madame, I will have to ask you to remain here while I report you for failing to show your identity card."

"Do that. And I will report you for your breach of etiquette toward a lady in the lobby of a grand hotel in a civilized European country. We will see which of us they put in jail. You will see which of us will go to a slave-labor camp."

I whisper, "Give him the card."

"Go!" she screams at the clerk. "Call the police, please. A man who failed to remove his hat to a lady in the elevator of the Jalta Hotel is now serving ten years in a uranium mine. A doorman who neglected to bow farewell

to a lady at the Hotel Esplanade is now in solitary confine-
ment without even toilet facilities. For what you have
done you will never again see your wife or your old
mother. Your children will grow up ashamed of their
father's name. Go. Go! I want my husband-to-be to see
what we do in this country to people without manners. I
want him to see that we do not smile here upon rudeness
to a Czech woman! Call the authorities—this minute! In
the meantime, we are going to have our breakfast. Come,
my dear one, my darling."

Taking my arm, she starts away, but not before the
clerk says, "There is a message, sir," and slips me an en-
velope. The note is handwritten on hotel stationery.

Dear Mr. Zuckerman,
I am a Czech student with a deep interest in American
writing. I have written a study of your fiction about which
I would like to talk to you. "The Luxury of Self-Analysis
As It Relates to American Economic Conditions." I will
meet with you here at the hotel anytime, if you will be
willing to receive me. Please leave word at the desk.
                                    Yours most respectfully,
                                    Oldrich Hrobek

The guests already taking breakfast watch over the rims
of their coffee cups while Olga vigorously declines to sit
at the corner table to which we have been shown by the

headwaiter. She points to a table beside the glass doors to the lobby. In English the headwaiter explains to me that this table is reserved.

"For breakfast?" she replies. "That is a fucking lie."

We are seated at the table by the lobby doors. I say, "What now, Olga? Tell me what's coming next."

"Please don't ask me about these things. They are just stupidities. I want eggs, please. Poached eggs. Nothing in life is as pure as a poached egg. If I don't eat I will faint."

"Tell me what was wrong with the first table."

"Bugged. Probably this table they bug too; probably all are bugged. Fuck it, I am too weak. Fuck the whole thing. Fuck it all. Teach me another one. I need this morning one that is really good."

"Where have you been all night?"

"You would not have me so I found some people who would. Call the waiter, please, or I will faint. I am going to faint. I am feeling sick. I am going to the loo to be sick."

I follow after her as she runs from the table, but when I reach the dining-room door, my way is blocked by a young man with a tiny chin beard; he is in a toggled loden coat and carrying a heavy briefcase. "Please," he says, his face only inches from mine—a face taut with panic and dreadful concern—"I have tried to reach you just now in your room. I am Oldrich Hrobek. You have received my note?"

"Only this minute," I say, watching Olga rush through the lobby to the ladies' room.

"You must leave Prague as soon as possible. You must not stay here. If you do not leave immediately, the authorities will harm you."

"Me? How do you know this?"

"Because they are building a case. I'm at Charles University. They questioned my professor, they questioned me."

"But I just got here. *What* case?"

"They told me you were on an espionage mission and to stay away from you. They said they will put you in jail for what you are doing here."

"For espionage?"

"Plotting against the Czech people. Plotting with troublemakers against the socialist system. You are an ideological saboteur—you must leave today."

"I'm an American citizen." I touch the billfold that holds not only my passport but my membership card in the American PEN Club, signed by the president, Jerzy Kosinski.

"Recently an American got off the train in Bratislava and was immediately put into jail for two months because he was mistaken for somebody else. He wasn't even the right person and that didn't get him out. An Austrian was taken from his hotel to prison a week ago and is to stand trial for anti-Czech activities. A West German journalist they drowned in the river. They said he was fishing and fell in. There are hard-line people who want to make an impression on the country. With you they can make an impression. This is what the police have told me. Many, many arrests are going to be made."

I hear very clearly the sound of the river splashing against the steep stone embankment outside of Klenek's palazzo.

"Because of me."

"Including you."

"Maybe they are just frightening you," I say, *my* heart galloping, galloping to burst.

"Mr. Zuckerman, I should not be in here. I must not be in here—but I am afraid to miss you. There is more. If you will walk to the railway station I will meet you there in five minutes. It is at the top of the main street—just to the left. You will see it. I will pretend to run into you outside the big station café. Please, they told my girlfriend the same thing. They questioned her at her job—about you."

"About me. You sure of all this?"

The student takes my hand and begins to pump it with exaggerated vigor. "It is an honor to meet you!" He speaks up so that all in the dining room who wish to can hear. "I am sorry I interrupted but I had to meet you. I can't help it if I am a silly fan! Goodbye, sir!"

Olga returns looking even worse than when she left. She also smells. "What a country." She falls heavily into her chair. "You cannot even throw up in the loo that someone does not write a report about it. There is a man waiting outside the cubicle when I am finished. He is listening to me from there all the time. 'Did you leave it clean?' he asks me. 'Yes,' I said, 'yes, I left it clean.' 'You shout, you scream, you have no respect for anything,' he tells me. 'Someone will come in after you and see your mess and blame it on me.' 'Go in then, go check,' I told him. And he did it. A man in a suit who can reason and think! He went in and inspected."

"Has anyone else bothered you?"

"They won't. They won't dare. Not if I am having breakfast with you. You are an international writer. They do not want to make trouble in the presence of an international writer."

"Then why did he bother about your identity card?"

"Because he is afraid not to. Everybody is afraid. I want to have my breakfast now with my international writer. I am hungry."

"Why don't we go somewhere else? I want to talk to you about something serious."

"You want to marry me. When?"

"Not quite yet. Come, let's go."

"No, we must not move. You must show them always that you are not afraid." When she picks up the menu I see she is trembling. "You must not leave," she says. "You must sit here and enjoy your breakfast and drink many cups of coffee, and then you must smoke a cigar. If they see you smoking a cigar, they will leave you alone."

"You put great stock in a single cigar."

"I know these Czech police—blow a little smoke in their faces and you'll see how brave they are. Last night I was in the pub, because you would not fuck me, and I am talking to the bartender about the hockey game and two men come in and sit down and begin to buy me drinks. Outside is parked a state limousine. We drink, they make loud jokes with the bartender, and then they show me the big car. They say to me, 'How would you like to take a ride in that? Not to question you, but to have a good time. We'll drink some more vodka and have a good time.' I thought, 'Don't be afraid, don't show them you are afraid.' So they drive me to an office building and we go inside and everything is dark, and when I say I can't see where I'm going one of them says they cannot turn the lights on. 'Everything,' he says, 'is observed where the lights are on.' You see, *he* is afraid. Now I know he is afraid too. Probably they should not even have the car, it belongs to their boss—something is wrong here. They open a door and we sit in a dark room and the two of them pour vodka for me, but they cannot even wait for me to drink, one of them takes out his prick and tries to pull me down on it. I feel him with my hand and I say to him, 'But it is technically impossible with this. You could never come with something so soft. Let me try his. No, his is technically impossible even more. I want to go. There is no fun here, and I can't even see anything. I want to go!' I begin to shout . . ."

The waiter returns to take the order. Poached eggs for two—as pure a thing as life has to offer.

After my three cups of coffee, Olga orders me a Cuban cigar and, at 8:30 a.m. Central European Time, I, who smoke a cigar once every decade and afterwards always wonder why, oblige her and light up.

"You must finish the cigar, Zuckerman. When freedom returns to Czechoslovakia, you will be made an honorary citizen for finishing that cigar. They will put a plaque outside this hotel about Zuckerman and his cigar."

"I'll finish the cigar," I say, dropping my voice, "if you give me Sisovsky's father's stories. The stories in Yiddish that Sisovsky left behind. I met your husband in New York. He asked me to come here and get the stories."

"That swine! That pig!"

"Olga, I didn't want to spring it on you out of the blue, but I've been advised not to hang around this country much longer."

"You met that monster in New York!"

"Yes."

"And the aging ingenue? You have met her too? And did she tell you how much she suffers from all the men at her feet? Did he tell you how with her it is never boring love-making—with her it is always like rape! This is why you are here, not for Kafka but for *him*?"

"Lower your voice. I'm taking those stories to America."

"So he can make money out of his dead father—in New York? So he can buy jewelry for her now in New York too?"

"He wants to publish his father's stories, in translation, in America."

"What—out of love? Out of *devotion*?"

"I don't know."

"*I* know! I know! That's why he left his mother, that's why he left me, that's why he left his child—because of all of this devoted love he has. Left us all for that whore they all rape. What's *she* doing in New York? Still playing Nina in *The Seagull*?"

"I wouldn't think so."

"Why not? She did here. Our leading Czech actress who ages but never grows up. Poor little star always in tears. And how much did he flatter you to make you believe that he was a man with love and devotion who cared only for the memory of his beloved father? How much did he flatter you about your books that you cannot see through what *both* of them are? *He* is why you come to Czechoslovakia—him? Because you took pity on two homeless Czechs? Take pity on *me*. I am at home, *and it is worse*!"

"I see that."

"And of course he told you the story of his father's death."

"He did."

" 'He shot my Jew, so I shot his.' "

"Yes."

"Well, that is another lie. It happened to another writer, who didn't even write in Yiddish. Who didn't have a wife or have a child. Sisovsky's father was killed in a bus accident. Sisovsky's father hid in the bathroom of a Gentile friend, hid there through the war from the Nazis, and his friend brought him cigarettes and whores."

"I find it hard believing that."

"Of course—because it's not as horrible a story! They all say their fathers were killed by the Nazis. By now even the sixteen-year-old girls know not to believe them. Only people like you, only a shallow, sentimental, American idiot Jew who thinks there is virtue in suffering!"

"You've got the wrong Jew—I think nothing of the sort. Let me have the manuscripts. What good do they do anybody here?"

"The good of not being there, doing good for him and that terrible actress! You cannot even *hear* her if you sit ten rows back. You could *never* hear her. She is a stinking actress who has ruined Chekhov for Prague for the last hundred years with all her stinking sensitive pauses, and now she will ruin Chekhov for New York. Nina? She should be playing Firs! He wants to live off of his father? The hell with him! Let him live off of his actress! If anybody can even hear her!"

* * *

59

I wait for Hrobek on a long bench in the corridor outside the railway café. Either because the student has himself waited and lost hope and gone home or because he has been taken into custody or because he was not a student but a provocateur got up in a wispy chin beard and worn loden coat, he is nowhere to be seen.

On the chance that he has decided to wait inside rather than under the scrutiny of the plainclothes security agents patrolling the halls, I enter the café and look around: a big dingy room, a dirty, airless, oppressive place. Patched, fraying tablecloths set with mugs of beer, and clinging to the mugs, men with close-cropped hair wearing gray-black work clothes, swathed in cigarette smoke and saying little. Off the night shift somewhere, or maybe tanking up on their way *to* work. Their faces indicate that not everybody heard the president when he went on television for three hours to ask the people not to drink so much.

Two waiters in soiled white jackets attend the fifty or so tables, both of them elderly and in no hurry. Since half of the country, by Olga's count, is employed in spying on the other half, chances are that one at least works for the police. (Am I getting drastically paranoid or am I getting the idea?) In German I order a cup of coffee.

The workmen at their beer remind me of Bolotka, a janitor in a museum now that he no longer runs his theater. "This," Bolotka explains, "is the way we arrange things now. The menial work is done by the writers and the teachers and the construction engineers, and the construction is run by the drunks and the crooks. Half a million people have been fired from their jobs. *Everything* is run by the drunks and the crooks. They get along better with the Russians." I imagine Styron washing glasses in a Penn Station barroom, Susan Sontag wrapping buns at a Broadway bakery, Gore Vidal bicycling salamis to school lunchrooms in Queens—I look at the filthy floor and see myself sweeping it.

Someone stares at me from a nearby table while I continue sizing up the floor and with it the unforeseen consequences of art. I am remembering the actress Eva Kalinova and how they have used Anne Frank as a whip to drive her from the stage, how the ghost of the Jewish saint has returned to haunt her as a demon. Anne Frank as a curse and a stigma! No, there's nothing that can't be done to a book, no cause in which even the most innocent of all books cannot be enlisted, not only by *them*, but by you and me. Had Eva Kalinova been born in New Jersey she too would have wished that Anne Frank had never died as she did; but coming, like Anne Frank, from the wrong continent at the wrong time, she could only wish that the Jewish girl and her little diary had never even existed.

Mightier than the *sword*? This place is proof that a book isn't as mighty as the mind of its most benighted reader.

When I get up to go, the young workman who'd been staring at me gets up and follows.

I board a trolley by the river, then jump off halfway to the museum where Bolotka is expecting me to pay him a visit. On foot, and with the help of a Prague map, I proceed to lose my way but also to shake my escort. By the time I reach the museum this seems to me a city that I've known all my life. The old-time streetcars, the barren shops, the soot-blackened bridges, the tunneled alleys and medieval streets, the people in a state of impervious heaviness, their faces shut down by solemnity, faces that appear to be on strike against life—this is the city I imagined during the war's worst years, when, as a Hebrew-school student of little more than nine, I went out after supper with my blue-and-white collection can to solicit from the neighbors for the Jewish National Fund. This is the city I imagined the Jews would buy when they had accumulated enough money for a homeland. I knew about Palestine and the hearty Jewish teenagers there reclaiming the desert and draining the swamps, but I also recalled, from our vague family chronicle, shadowy, cramped streets where the innkeepers and distillery workers who were our Old World forebears had dwelled apart, as strangers, from the notorious Poles—and so, what I privately pictured the Jews able to afford with the nickels and dimes I collected was a used city, a broken city, a city so worn and grim that nobody else would even put in a bid. It would go for a song, the owner delighted to be rid of it before it completely caved in. In this used city, one would hear endless stories being told—on benches in the park, in kitchens at night, while waiting your turn at the grocery or over the clothesline in the yard, anxious tales of harassment and flight, stories of fantastic endurance and pitiful collapse. What was to betoken a Jewish homeland to an impressionable, emotional nine-year-old child, highly susceptible to the emblems of pathos, was, first, the overpowering oldness of the homes, the centuries of deterioration that had made the property so cheap, the leaky pipes and moldy walls and rotting timbers and smoking stoves and simmering cabbages souring the air of the semidark stairwells; second were the stories, all the telling and listening to be done, their infinite interest in their own existence, the fascination with their alarming plight, the mining and refining of *tons* of these stories—the national industry of the Jewish homeland, if not the sole means of production (if not the sole source of satisfaction), the construction of narrative out of the exertions of survival; third were the jokes—because beneath the ordeal of perpetual melancholia and the tremendous strain of just getting through, a joke is always lurking somewhere, a derisory portrait, a scathing crack, a joke which builds with subtle self-savaging to the uproarious punch line, "And this is what suffering does!" What you smell are centuries and what you hear are voices and what you see are Jews, wild with lament and rippling with amusement, their voices tremulous with rancor and vibrating with pain, a choral society proclaiming vehemently, "Do you believe it? Can you imagine it?" even as they affirm with every wizardly trick in the book, by a thousand acoustical fluctuations of tempo, tone, inflection, and pitch, "Yet this is exactly what happened!" That such things can happen—there's the moral of the stories—that such things happen to me, to him, to her, to you, to us. That is the national anthem of the Jewish homeland. By all rights, when you hear someone there begin telling a story—when you see the Jewish faces mastering anxiety and feigning innocence and registering astonishment at their own fortitude—you ought to stand and put your hand to your heart.

Here where the literary culture is held hostage, the art of narration flourishes by mouth. In Prague, stories aren't simply stories; it's what they have instead of life. Here they have become their stories, in lieu of being permitted to be anything else. Storytelling is the form their resistance has taken against the coercion of the powers-that-be.

I say nothing to Bolotka of the sentiments stirred up by my circuitous escape route, or the association it's inspired between my ancestors' Poland, his Prague tenement, and the Jewish Atlantis of an American childhood dream. I only explain why I'm late. "I was followed from the train station onto the trolley. I shook him before I got here. I hope I wasn't wrong to come anyway." I describe the student Hrobek and show Bolotka his note. "The note was given to me by a hotel clerk who I think is a cop."

After reading it twice he says, "Don't worry, they were only frightening him and his teacher."

"If so, they succeeded. In frightening me too."

"Whatever the reason, it is not to build a case against you. They do this to everyone. It is one of the laws of power, the spreading of general distrust. It is one of several basic techniques of *adjusting* people. But they cannot touch you. That would be pointless, even by Prague standards. A regime can only be so stupid, and then the other side comes back into power. Here *you* frighten *them*. A student should understand that. He is not enrolled in the right courses."

"Coming to the hotel then, he made things worse for himself—for his teacher too, if all this is true."

"I can't say. There is probably more about this boy that we don't know. The student and his teacher are who they are interested in, not you. You are not responsible for the boy's bad judgment."

"He was young. He wanted to help."

"Don't be tender about his martyr complex. And don't credit the secret police with so much. Of course the hotel clerk is a cop. Everybody is in that hotel. But the police are like literary critics—of what little they see, they get most wrong anyway. They *are* the literary critics. Our literary criticism is police criticism. As for the boy, he is right now back in his room with his pants off, boasting to his girl friend about saving your life."

Bolotka is padded out beneath his overalls with a scruffy,

repulsive reddish fur vest that could be the hair off his own thick hide, and consequently looks even more barbarous, more feral, at work than he did at play. He looks, in *this* enclosure, like one of the zoo's larger beasts, a bison or a bear. We are in a freezing storage room about twice as big as an ordinary clothes closet and a third the size of his living quarters. Both of us are sipping slivovitz-larded tea from his mug, I to calm down and Bolotka to warm up. The cartons stacked to the ceiling contain his cleanser, his toilet tissue, his floor polish, his lye; ranged along the walls are the janitor's buffing machine, ladder, and collection of brooms. In one corner, the corner Bolotka calls "my office," are a low stool, a gooseneck lamp, and the electric kettle to boil the water into which to dip his tea bag and pour the brandy. He reads here, writes, hides, sleeps, here on a scrap of carpet between the push broom and the buffer he entertains sixteen girls, though never, he informs me, in so tiny a space, all of them at one time. "More than two girls and there's no room for my prick."

"And there's nothing to be done about this boy's warning? I'm relying on you, Rudolf. When you come to New York I'll see you're not mugged in Central Park by going to take a leak there at 3 a.m. I expect the same consideration from you here. Am I in danger?"

"I was once briefly in jail, waiting to stand trial, Nathan. Before the trial began, they released me. It was too ridiculous even for them. They told me I had committed a crime against the state: in my theater, the heroes were always laughing when they should be crying, and this was a crime. I was an ideological saboteur. Stalinist criticism, which once existed in this country until it became a laughingstock, always reproached characters for not being moral and setting a good example. When a hero's wife died on the stage, which was often happening in my theater, he had to sob a lot to please Stalin. And Stalin of course knew quite well what it was when one's wife died. He himself killed three wives and in killing them he was always sobbing. Well, when I was in jail, you realized when you woke up where you were, and you began cursing. You could hear them cursing in their cells, all the professional criminals, all the pimps and murderers and thieves. I was only a young man, but I began cursing too. The thing I learned was not to stop cursing, never to stop cursing, not when you are in a prison. Forget this note. To hell with these people and their warnings. Anything you want to do in Prague, anything you want to see in Prague, anyone you want to fuck in Prague, you tell me and I arrange it. There is still some pleasure for a stranger in *Mitteleuropa*. I hesitate to say Prague is 'gay,' but sometimes these days it can be very amusing."

Afternoon. Olga's garret atop Klenek's palazzo. A pinnacle of Prague's castle blurrily visible through the leaded window. Olga in her robe on the bed. Witchy, very whit-ish, even without the makeup. I pace, wearing my coat, wondering why these stories must be retrieved. Why am I forcing the issue? What's the motive here? Is this a pas-sionate struggle for those marvelous stories or a renewal of the struggle toward self-caricature? Still the son, still the child, in strenuous pursuit of the father's loving re-sponse? (Even when the father is Sisovsky's?) Suppose the stories aren't even marvelous, that I only long for that —the form taken by my touha. *Why am I saying to my-self,* "Do not let yourself be stopped"? *Why be drawn further along, the larger the obstacles? That's okay writ-ing a book, that's what it* is *to write a book, but would it be so hard to convince myself that I am stupidly endowing these stories with a significance that they can't begin to have? How consequential can they be? If their genius could really astound us they would somehow have sur-faced long ago. The author's purpose wasn't to be read anyway, but to write for no necessity other than his own. Why not let him have it his way, rather than yours or Sisovsky's? Think of all that his stories will be spared if instead of wrenching his fiction out of oblivion, you just turn around and go . . . Yet I stay. In the old parables about the spiritual life, the hero searches for a kind of holi-ness, or holy object, or transcendence, boning up on magic practices as he goes off hunting after his higher being, getting help from crones and soothsayers, donning masks*

—well, this is the mockery of that parable, that parable the idealization of this farce. The soul sinking into ridiculousness even while it strives to be saved. Enter Zuckerman, a serious person.

O. You're afraid to marry an alcoholic? I would love you so, I wouldn't drink.

Z. And you give me the stories as your dowry.

O. Maybe.

Z. Where are the stories?

O. I don't know where.

Z. He left them with you—you must know. His mother came to you and tried to get them, and you showed her photographs of his mistresses. That's what he told me.

O. Don't be sentimental. They were pictures of their cunts. Do you think they were so different from mine? You think theirs were prettier? Here. (*Opens her robe*) Look. Theirs were exactly the same.

Z. You have all your things here?

O. I don't have *things*. In the sense that you Americans have *things*, I don't have *anything*.

Z. Do you have the stories here?

O. Let's go to the American Embassy and get married.

Z. And then you'll give me the stories.

O. More than likely. Tell me, what are you getting out of this?

Z. A headache. A terrific headache and a look at your cunt. That's about it.

O. Ah, you are doing it for idealistic reasons. You do it for literature. For altruism. You are a great American, a great humanitarian, and a great Jew.

Z. I'll give you ten thousand dollars.

O. Ten thousand dollars? I could use ten thousand dollars. But there's no amount of money you could give me. Nothing would be worth it.

Z. And you don't care about literature.

O. I care about literature. I love literature. But not as much as I love to keep these things from him. And from her. You really think I am going to give you these stories so he can keep her in jewels? You really think that in New York he's going to publish these stories under his father's name?

Z. Why shouldn't he?

O. Why should he—what's in it for *him*? He'll publish them under his own name. His beloved father is dead now ten times over. He'll publish the stories under his own name and become famous in America like all you Jews.

Z. I didn't know you were an anti-Semite.

O. Only because of Sisovsky. If you would marry me, I would change. Am I so unattractive to you that you don't want to marry me? Is his aging ingenue more attractive to you than I am?

Z. I can't really believe you mean all this. You're an impressive character, Olga. In your own way you're fighting to live.

O. Then marry me, if I am so impressive from fighting to live. You're not married to anyone else. What are you afraid of—that I'll take your millions?

Z. Look, you want a ticket out of Czechoslovakia?

O. Maybe I want you.

Z. What if I get someone to marry you. He'll come here, get you to America, and when you divorce him I'll give you ten thousand dollars.

O. Am I so revolting that I can only marry one of your queer friends?

Z. Olga, how do I wrest these stories from you? Just tell me.

O. Zuckerman, if you were such an idealist about literature as you want me to be, if you would make great sacrifices for literature as you expect me to make, we would have been married twenty minutes already.

Z. Is whatever Sisovsky did so awful that his dead father must suffer too?

O. When the stories are published in New York without the father's name, the father will suffer more, believe me.

Z. Suppose that doesn't happen. Suppose I make that impossible.

O. *You* will outtrick Zdenek?

Z. I'll contact *The New York Times*. Before seeing Zdenek, I'll tell them the whole story of these stories. They'll run an article about them. Suppose I do that as soon as I'm back.

O. So *that's* what you get out of it! *That's* your idealism! The marvelous Zuckerman brings from behind the Iron Curtain two hundred unpublished Yiddish stories written by a victim of a Nazi bullet. You will be a hero to the Jews and to literature and to all of the Free World. On top of all your millions of dollars and millions of girls, you will win the American Prize for Idealism about Literature. And what will happen to me? I will go to prison for smuggling a manuscript to the West.

Z. They won't know the stories came through you.

O. But they know already that I have them. They know everything I have. They have a list of everything that *everybody* has. You get the idealism prize, he gets the royalties, she gets the jewelry, and I get seven years. For the sake of literature.

Here she gets up from the bed, goes to the dresser, and removes from the top drawer a deep box for chocolates. I untie the ribbon on the box. Inside, hundreds of pages of unusually thick paper, rather like the heavy waxed paper that oily foodstuffs used to be wrapped in at the grocery. The ink is black, the margins perfect, the Yiddish script is sharp and neat. None of the stories seems longer than five or six pages. I can't read them.

O. (*Back in bed*) You don't have to give me money. You don't have to find me a queer to be my husband. (*Beginning to cry*) You don't even have to fuck me, if I am such an unattractive woman. To be fucked is the only freedom left in this country. To fuck and to be fucked is all we have left that they cannot stop, but you do not have to fuck me, if I am such an unattractive woman compared to the American girls. He can even print the stories in his own name, your friend Sisovsky. The hell with it. The hell with everything. In spite of the charm with which he seduced you, with which he seduces *everybody*, he can be quite vicious—do you know? There is great brutality in your Sisovsky. Did he tell you about all his doubts—his tragic doubts? What shit! Before Zdenek left Prague, we measured personal vanity here in millisisovskys. Zdenek will survive in America. He is human in the worst sense of the word. Zdenek will flourish, thanks to his dead father. So will she. And in return, I want nothing. Only that when he asks you how much did you have to give her, how much money and how many fucks, you will do me one favor: tell him you had to give me nothing. Tell *her*.

At the hotel, two plainclothes policemen come to the room and confiscate the candy box full of Yiddish manuscript within fifteen minutes of my return. They are accompanied by the hotel clerk who'd earlier in the day handed me Hrobek's note. "They wish to examine your belongings, sir," he tells me—"they say somebody has mislaid something which you may have picked up by mistake." "My belongings are none of their business." "I'm afraid you are wrong. That is precisely their business." As the police begin their search I ask him, "And you, what's your business?" "I merely work at the reception desk. It is not only the intellectual who may be sent down to the mines if he does not cooperate with the present regime, the hotel clerk can be demoted as well. As one of our famous dissidents has said, a man who speaks only the truth, 'There is always a lower rung under the feet of every citizen on the ladder of the state.' " I demand to be allowed to telephone the American Embassy, and not so as to arrange a wedding. I am told instead to pack my bags. I will be driven to the airport and put on the next plane out of Prague. I am no longer welcome as a visitor in Czechoslovakia. "I want to speak to the American ambassador. They cannot confiscate my belongings. There are no grounds on which to expel me from this country. " "Sir, though it may appear to you that ardent supporters of this regime are few and far between, there are also those, like these two gentlemen, who have no trouble believing that what they do is right, correct, and necessary. Brutally necessary. I am afraid that any further delay is going to cause them to be less lenient than you would like." "What the box contains is simply manuscript—stories written by somebody who's been dead now thirty years, fiction about a world that no longer even exists. It is no possible threat to anyone." "I am grateful, sir, in times like these, still to be able to support my family. There is nothing a clerk in a Prague hotel can do for any writer, living or dead." When I demand for the third time to speak to the Embassy, I am told that if I do not immediately pack my bags and prepare to leave, I will be arrested and taken to jail. "How do I know," I ask, "that they won't take me to jail anyway?" "I suppose," the clerk replies, "that you will have to trust them."

Either Olga had a change of heart and called the cops, or else they called on her. Klenek's is bugged, everyone says so. I just cannot believe that she and the hotel clerk work for the same boss, but maybe that's because I *am* a shallow, sentimental, American idiot Jew.

At the desk the police wait while I charge my bills to the Diners Club and then I am accompanied by them to a black limousine. One policeman sits up front with the driver and the candy box, and the other in the back with me and a bulky, bespectacled, elderly man who introduces himself gruffly as Novak. Soft, fine white hair like the fluff of a dry dandelion. Otherwise a man made of meat. He is no charmer like the hotel clerk.

Out beyond the heavy city traffic I am unable to tell if we really are on the airport road. Can they be taking me to jail in a limo? I always seem to end up in these large black cars. The dashboard says this one is a Tatra 603.

"Sie sprechen Deutsch, nicht wahr?" Novak asks me.
"Etwas."

"Kennen sie Fraulein Betty MacDonald?"

We continue in German. "I don't," I say.

"You *don't*?"

"No."

"You don't know Miss Betty MacDonald?"

I can't stop thinking how badly this can still turn out—
or, alternatively, that I could honorably have abandoned
the mission once I saw the dangers were real. Because
Sisovsky claimed to be my counterpart from the world
that my own fortunate family had eluded didn't mean I
had to prove him right by rushing in to change places. I
assume his fate and he assumes mine—wasn't that sort of
his idea from the start? *When I came to New York I said
to Eva, "I am a relative of this great man."*

Guilty of conspiring against the Czech people with
somebody named Betty MacDonald. Thus I conclude my
penance.

"Sorry," I say, "I don't know her."

"But," says Novak, "she is the author of *The Egg and I*."

"Ah. Yes. About a farm—wasn't it? I haven't read it
since I was a schoolboy."

Novak is incredulous. "But it is a masterpiece."

"Well, I can't say it's considered a masterpiece in America. I'd be surprised if in America anybody under thirty
has even heard of *The Egg and I*."

"I cannot believe this."

"It's true. It was popular in the forties, a bestseller, a movie, but books like that come and go. Surely you have the same thing here."

"That is a tragedy. And what has happened to Miss Betty MacDonald?"

"I have no idea."

"Why does something like this happen in America to a writer like Miss MacDonald?"

"I don't think even Miss MacDonald expected her book to endure forever."

"You have not answered me. You avoid the question. Why does this happen in America?"

"I don't know."

I search in vain for signs to the airport.

Novak is suddenly angry. "There is no paranoia here about writers."

"I didn't say there was."

"I am a writer. I am a successful writer. Nobody is paranoid about me. Ours is the most literate country in Europe. Our people love books. I have in the Writers' Union dozens of writers, poets, novelists, playwrights, and no one is paranoid about them. No, it isn't writers who fall under our suspicion in Czechoslovakia. In this small country the writers have a great burden to bear: they must not only make the country's literature, they must be the touchstone for general decency and public conscience.

They occupy a high position in our national life because they are people who live beyond reproach. Our writers are loved by their readers. The country looks to them for moral leadership. No, it is those who stand outside of the common life, that is who we all fear. And we are right to."

I can imagine what he contributes to his country's literature: *Still more humorous Novakian tales about the crooked little streets of Old Prague, stories that poke fun at all citizens, high and low, and always with spicy folk humor and mischievous fantasy. A must for the sentimental at holiday time.*

"You are with the Writers' Union?" I ask.

My ignorance ignites a glower of contempt. I dare to think of myself as an educated person and know nothing of the meaning of the Tatra 603? He says, *"Ich bin der Kulturminister."*

So he is the man who administers the culture of Czechoslovakia, whose job is to bring the aims of literature into line with the aims of society, to make literature less *inefficient*, from a social point of view. You write, if you even can here, into the teeth of this.

"Well," I say, "it's kind of you personally to see me out, Mr. Minister. This is the road to the airport? Frankly I don't recognize it."

"You should have taken the time to come to see me when you first arrived. It would have been worth your while. I would have made you realize what the common life is in Czechoslovakia. You would understand that the ordinary Czech citizen does not think like the sort of people you have chosen to meet. He does not behave like them and he does not admire them. The ordinary Czech is repelled by such people. Who are they? Sexual perverts. Alienated neurotics. Bitter egomaniacs. They seem to you courageous? You find it thrilling, the price they pay for their great art? Well, the ordinary hardworking Czech who wants a better life for himself and his family is not so thrilled. He considers them malcontents and parasites and outcasts. At least their blessed Kafka knew he was a freak, recognized that he was a misfit who could never enter into a healthy, ordinary existence alongside his countrymen. But *these* people? Incorrigible deviants who propose to make their moral outlook the norm. The worst is that left to themselves, left to run free to do as they wish, these people would destroy this country. I don't even speak of their moral degeneracy. With this they only make themselves and their families miserable, and destroy the lives of their children. I am thinking of their political stupidity. Do you know what Brezhnev told Dubček when he flew our great reform leader to the Soviet Union back in '68? Brezhnev sent several hundred thousand troops to Prague to get Mr. Dubček to come to his senses about his great program of reforms. But to be on the safe side with this genius, he had him taken one evening from his office and flown to the Soviet Union for a little talk."

To the Soviet Union. Suppose they put me aboard Aeroflot, suppose that's the next plane out of Prague. Suppose they keep me *here*. *As Nathan Zuckerman awoke one morning from uneasy dreams he found himself transformed in his bed into a sweeper of floors in a railway café. There are petitions for him to sign, or not to sign; there are questions for him to answer, or not to answer; there are enemies to despise, there are friends to console, mail doesn't reach him, a phone they withhold, there are informers, breakdowns, betrayals, threats, there is for him even a strange brand of freedom—invalidated by the authorities, a superfluous person with no responsibilities and nothing to do, he has the kind of good times you have in Dante's Inferno; and finally, to really break him on the rack of farce, there is Novak squatting over the face of culture: when he awakens in the morning, realizes where he is and remembers what he's turned into, he begins to curse and doesn't stop cursing.*

I speak up. "I am an American citizen, Mr. Minister. I want to know what's going on here. Why these policemen? I have committed no crime."

"You have committed several crimes, each punishable by sentences of up to twenty years in jail."

"I demand to be taken to the American Embassy."

"Let me tell you what Brezhnev told Mr. Dubček that Mr. Bolotka neglected to say while elucidating on the size of his sexual organ. One, he would deport our Czech intelligentsia en masse to Siberia; two, he would turn Czechoslovakia into a Soviet republic; three, he would make Russian the language in the schools. In twenty years nobody would even remember that such a country as Czechoslovakia had ever existed. This is not the United States of America where every freakish thought is a fit subject for writing, where there is no such thing as propriety, decorum, or shame, nor a decent respect for the morality of the ordinary, hardworking citizen. This is a small country of fifteen million, dependent as it has always been upon the goodwill of a mighty neighbor. Those Czechs who inflame the anger of our mighty neighbor are not patriots—*they are the enemy.* There is nothing praiseworthy about them. The men to praise in this country are men like my own little father. You want to respect somebody in Czechoslovakia? Respect my father! I admire my old father and with good reason. I am *proud* of this little man."

And your father, is he proud of you and does he think you are all you should be? Certainly Novak is all he thinks he should be—perceives perfectly what *everybody* should be. One conviction seems to follow from the other.

"My father is a simple machinist, now long retired, and do you know how he has made his contribution to the survival of Czech culture and the Czech people and the Czech language—even of Czech literature? A contribution greater than your lesbian whore who when she opens her legs for an American writer represents to him the authentic Czech spirit. Do you know how my father has expressed his love of country all his life? In 1937 he praised Masaryk and the Republic, praised Masaryk as our great national hero and saviour. When Hitler came in he praised Hitler. After the war he praised Beneš when he was elected prime minister. When Stalin threw Beneš out, he praised Stalin and our great leader Gottwald. Even when Dubček came in, for a few minutes he praised Dubček. But now that Dubček and his great reform government are gone, he would not dream of praising them. Do you know what he tells me now? Do you want to hear the political philosophy of a true Czech patriot who has lived in this little country for eighty-six years, who made a decent and comfortable little home for his wife and his four children, and who lives now in dignified retirement, enjoying, as he has every right to enjoy, his pipe, and his grandchildren, and his pint of beer, and the company of his dear old friends? He says to me, 'Son, if someone called Jan Hus nothing but a dirty Jew, I would agree.' These are our people who represent the true Czech spirit—*these are our realists*! People who understand what *necessity* is. People who do not sneer at order and see only the worst in everything. People who know to distinguish between what remains possible in a little country like ours and what is a stupid, maniacal delusion—*people who know how to submit decently to their historical misfortune! These* are the people to whom we owe the survival of our beloved land, and not to alienated, degenerate, egomaniacal artistes!"

Customs a breeze—my possessions combed over so many times while still in the dresser at the hotel that my bags are put right on through at the weigh-in counter and I'm accompanied by the plainclothesmen straight to passport control. I have not been arrested, I will not be tried, convicted, and jailed; Dubček's fate isn't to be mine, nor is Bolotka's, Olga's, or Zdenek Sisovsky's. I am to be placed on board the Swissair flight bound nonstop for Geneva, and from there I'll catch a plane for New York.

Swissair. The most beautiful word in the English language.

Yet it makes you furious to be thrown out, once the fear has begun to subside. "What could entice me to this desolate country," says K., "except the wish to stay here?" —here where there's no nonsense about purity and goodness, where the division is not that easy to discern between the heroic and the perverse, where every sort of repression foments a parody of freedom and the suffering of their historical misfortune engenders in its imaginative victims these clownish forms of human despair—here where they're careful to remind the citizens (in case anybody gets any screwy ideas) "the phenomenon of alienation is not approved of from above." In this nation of narrators I'd only just begun hearing all their stories; I'd only just begun to sense myself shedding *my* story, as wordlessly as possible snaking away from the narrative encasing me. Worst of all, I've lost that astonishingly real candy box stuffed with the stories I came to Prague to retrieve. Another Jewish writer who might have been is not going to be; his imagination won't leave even the faintest imprint and no one else's imagination will be imprinted on his, neither the policemen practicing literary criticism nor the meaning-mad students living only for art.

Of course my theatrical friend Olga, for whose routine I have been playing straight man, wasn't necessarily making Prague mischief when she disclosed that the Yiddish author's war was endured in a bathroom, surviving on cigarettes and whores, and that when he perished it was under a bus. And maybe it *was* Sisovsky's plan to pretend in America that the father's achievement was his. Yet even if Sisovsky's stories, those told to me in New York, were tailored to exploit the listener's sentiments, a strategically devised fiction to set me in motion, that still doesn't mitigate the sense of extraneous irrelevancy I now feel. Another assault upon a world of significance degenerating into a personal fiasco, and this time in a record forty-eight hours! No, one's story isn't a skin to be shed—it's inescapable, one's body and blood. You go on pumping it out till you die, the story veined with the themes of your life, the ever-recurring story that's at once your invention and the invention of you. To be transformed into a cultural eminence elevated by the literary deeds he performs would not seem to be my fate. A forty-minute valedictory from the Minister of Culture on artistic deviance and filial respect is all I have been given to carry home. They must have seen me coming.

I also have to wonder if Novak's narrative is any less an invention than Sisovsky's. The true Czech patriot to whom the land owes its survival may well be another character out of mock-autobiography, yet another fabricated father manufactured to serve the purposes of a storytelling son. As if the core of existence isn't fantastic enough, still more fabulation to embellish the edges.

A sleek, well-groomed, dark-eyed man, slight, sultry, a Persian-looking fellow of about my own age, is standing back of the passport desk, alongside the on-duty army officer whose job is to process foreigners out of the country. His hourglass blue suit looks to have been styled specially for him in Paris or Rome—nothing like the suits I've seen around here, either in the streets or at the orgies. A man of European sophistication, no less a ladies' man, I would guess, than Novak's whoremaster Bolotka. Ostentatiously in English he asks to see the gentleman's papers. I pass them to the soldier, who in turn hands them to him. He reads over the biographical details—to determine, you see, if I am fiction or fact—then, sardonically, examining me as though I am now utterly transparent, comes so close that I smell the oil in his hair and the skin bracer that he's used after shaving. "Ah yes," he says, his magnitude in the scheme of things impressed upon me with that smile whose purpose is to make one uneasy, the smile of power

85

being benign, "Zuckerman the Zionist agent," he says, and returns my American passport. "An honor," he informs me, "to have entertained you here, sir. Now back to the little world around the corner."

OPERATION SHYLOCK

In this tour de force of fact and fiction, Philip Roth meets a man who may or may not be Philip Roth. Because *someone* with that name has been touring the State of Israel, promoting a bizarre exodus in reverse, Roth decides to stop him—even if that means impersonating his impersonator.
Fiction/Literature/0-679-75029-0

THE PROFESSOR OF DESIRE

As Philip Roth follows Professor David Kepesh from the domesticity of childhood into the vast wilderness of erotic possibility, from a ménage à trois in London to the throes of loneliness in New York, he creates an intelligent, affecting, and hilarious novel about the dilemma of pleasure: where we seek it; why we flee it; and how we struggle to make a truce between dignity and desire.
Fiction/Literature/0-679-74900-4

THE BREAST

Professor David Kepesh wakes up one morning to find that he has been transformed into a 155-pound female breast. What follows is an exploration of the full implications of Kepesh's metamorphosis—a daring, heretical book that brings us face to face with the intrinsic strangeness of sex and subjectivity.
Fiction/Literature/0-679-74901-2

MY LIFE AS A MAN

At the heart of Philip Roth's novel on sexual animus is a portrait of the marriage between Peter Tarnopol, a gifted young novelist, and Maureen, the woman who wants to be his muse but functions as his nemesis. Their union is based on fraud and sustained by moral blackmail but is so perversely durable that, long after Maureen's death, Peter is still trying futilely to write his way out of it.

Fiction/Literature/0-679-74827-X

GOODBYE, COLUMBUS
and Five Short Stories

In Philip Roth's National Book Award–winning first novel, Radcliffe-bound Brenda Patimkin initiates Neil Klugman of Newark into a new and unsettling society of sex, leisure, and loss. Also included in this volume are five classic short stories.

Fiction/Literature/0-679-74826-1

PORTNOY'S COMPLAINT

Philip Roth's classic novel with a new afterword by the author for the twenty-fifth-anniversary edition. "Simply one of the two or three funniest works in American fiction" (*Chicago Sun-Times*).

Fiction/Literature/0-679-75645-0

WHEN SHE WAS GOOD

Wounded by life and wild with righteousness, a Midwestern girl in the 1940s sets out to make the men of her world do their duty by their wives and children.

Fiction/Literature/0-679-75925-5

THE GREAT AMERICAN NOVEL

In this ribald, richly imagined, and wickedly satiric novel, Philip Roth turns baseball's status as national pastime and myth into an occasion for unfettered picaresque farce, replete with heroism and perfidy, ebullient word play and a cast of characters that includes the House Un-American Activities Committee.

Fiction/Literature/0-679-74906-3

THE GHOST WRITER

The story of a budding American writer, Nathan Zuckerman, who meets and falls in love with Anne Frank in New England—or so he thinks.

Fiction/Literature/0-679-74898-9

ZUCKERMAN UNBOUND

In *Zuckerman Unbound*, the notorious novelist Nathan Zuckerman retreats from his oldest friends, breaks his marriage to a virtuous woman, and damages, perhaps irreparably, his affectionate connection to his younger brother and family . . . and all because of his great good fortune!

Fiction/Literature/0-679-74899-7

THE ANATOMY LESSON

The hilarious story of Nathan Zuckerman, the famous forty-year-old writer, who decides to give it all up and become a doctor—and a pornographer—instead.

Fiction/Literature/0-679-74902-2